Jane Clarke & Britta Teckentrup

LEAP FROG

nosy crow

The three big frogs in this jungle pool are all making lots of noise. But one small frog is not joining in. Can you spot him?

Well done! You've found **Felix.**

Felix is a tree frog and tree frogs don't
live in ponds like most other frogs.
They live **high** in the jungle trees.
Poor Felix is **lost.**

But wait . . .
Did you hear that?

**Plip! Plop!
Plip! Splosh!**

What's that noise?

Felix looks a bit worried, doesn't he?
But there's nothing to be scared of.
Let's turn the page and show him . . .

It's just a friendly **turtle** popping up
to watch the sunset.

She gave Felix such a fright he leaped
off to hide behind a bumpy rock!
Can you **point** to him?

Here he is!

Say, "Don't worry, little frog,
there's nothing to be scared of."

**Pitter-patter!
Rustle! Rustle!**

What's that noise?

It's just a shiny **beetle** walking
across the leaves.

But Felix isn't stopping to find out
what it was. He has leaped away
again — off down the path.

Don't worry, little frog, there's
nothing to be scared of.

**Crack! Crunch!
Clatter!**

What's **that** noise?

It's just the cheeky **monkeys**
nibbling their nutty night-time snacks
and throwing down the shells.

Poor Felix. He's a very **jumpy** frog, isn't he? He has leaped off again.

Don't worry, little frog, there's nothing to be scared of.

I hope we don't hear any **more** strange sounds.

Swooshy-whooshy!
Swooshy-whooshy!

Uh-oh! What's that noise?

Oh! It's a slithery **snake** searching for a tasty bite to eat.

Quick! Clap your hands together and shout, **"Shoo, slithery snake!"**

Well done! You scared the snake away.

That was a **little** bit scary!
Perhaps the jungle floor **is** a bit
dangerous for a tiny tree frog
after all. Maybe Felix would be
safer in the trees?

It looks as if Felix has had the
same idea. He's starting to climb.

up he goes!

up . . .

Up . . .

But . . .

Rat-a-tat-tat!
Rat-a-tat-tat!

Now, what's **that** noise?

Phew! It's only a busy woodpecker tap-tapping on the tree trunk.

He's nothing to be scared of. But Felix is climbing faster now, up the tall tree.

It's a **very** tall tree,
but Felix's sticky toes
hold on tight to help
him climb.

Let's **count** the branches
to help him go faster
and faster.

. . . 10!

At last! He has reached the top of the tree.
Say, "Well done, Felix."

But . . .

Hop! Hop! Hop!

Oh no! What's that noise?

It's getting closer . . . and closer . . . and closer . . .

Someone's coming!

We need to warn Felix!

Quickly shout, **"Leap, frog!"**

Ah! Felix knows there's nothing
to be scared of now . . .

It's his daddy!

It's time for bed and Felix's daddy has
come to settle him down to sleep.

Now the jungle is peaceful and quiet.

Whisper, **"Sweet dreams, little frog,"**
and very quietly close the book.

First published 2019
by Nosy Crow Ltd
The Crow's Nest, 14 Baden Place
Crosby Row, London SE1 1YW
www.nosycrow.com

ISBN 978 1 78800 311 7

Nosy Crow and associated logos
are trademarks and/or
registered trademarks of
Nosy Crow Ltd

Text © Jane Clarke 2019
Illustrations © Britta Teckentrup 2019

The right of Jane Clarke to be identified
as the author of this work and of Britta Teckentrup
to be identified as the illustrator of this work
has been asserted.

A CIP catalogue record for this book is available
from the British Library.

Printed in China

Papers used by Nosy Crow are made from
wood grown in sustainable forests.

1 3 5 7 9 8 6 4 2